CU00841531

This book
belongs to

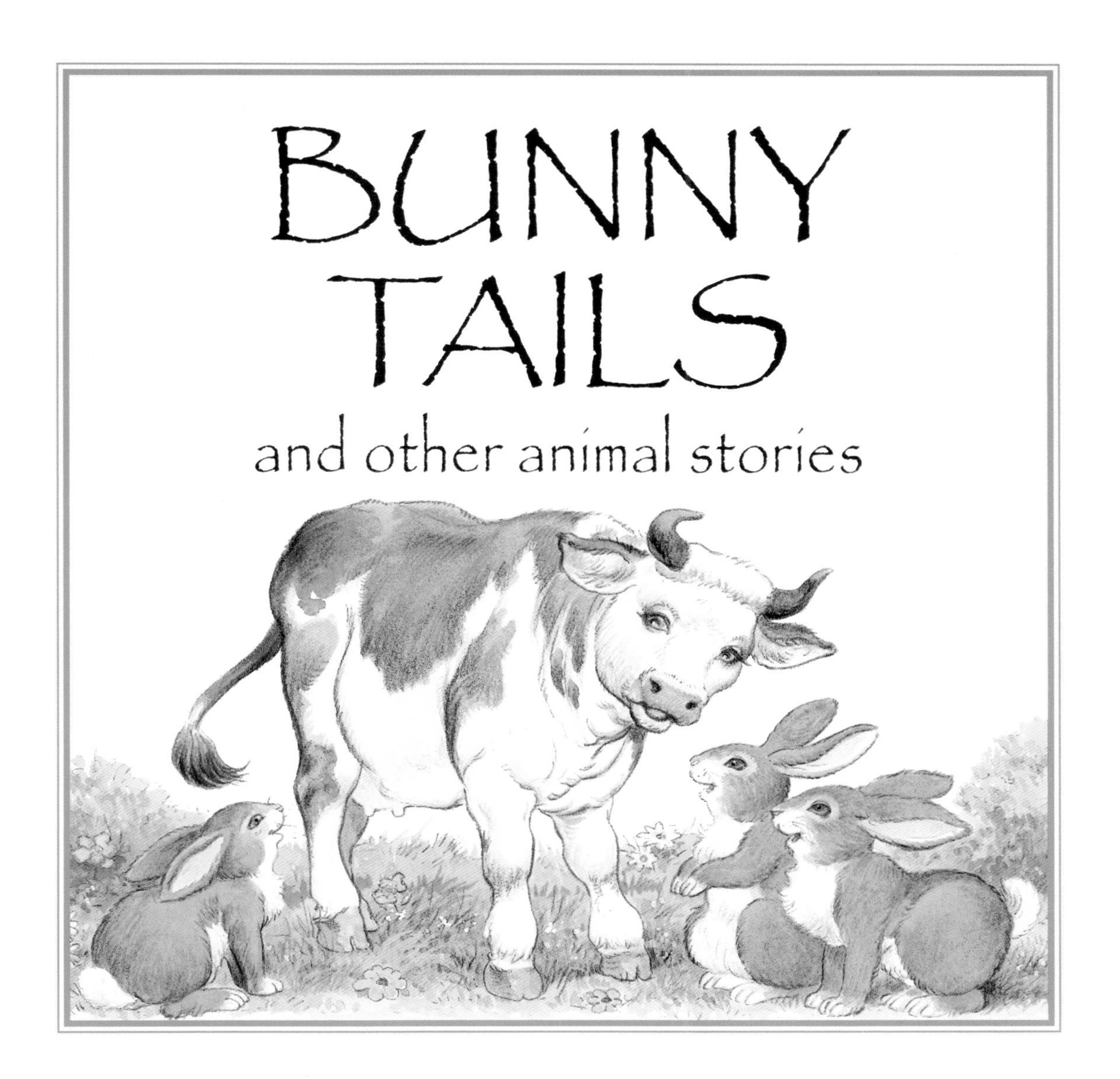

p

This is a Parragon book
This edition published in 2001

Parragon
Queen Street House, 4 Queen Street,
Bath, BA1 1HE, UK

Produced by The Templar Company plc
Pippbrook Mill, London Road, Dorking,
Surrey, RH4 1JE, UK

Designed by Kilnwood Graphics

Printed and bound in Spain

ISBN 0-75256-676-2

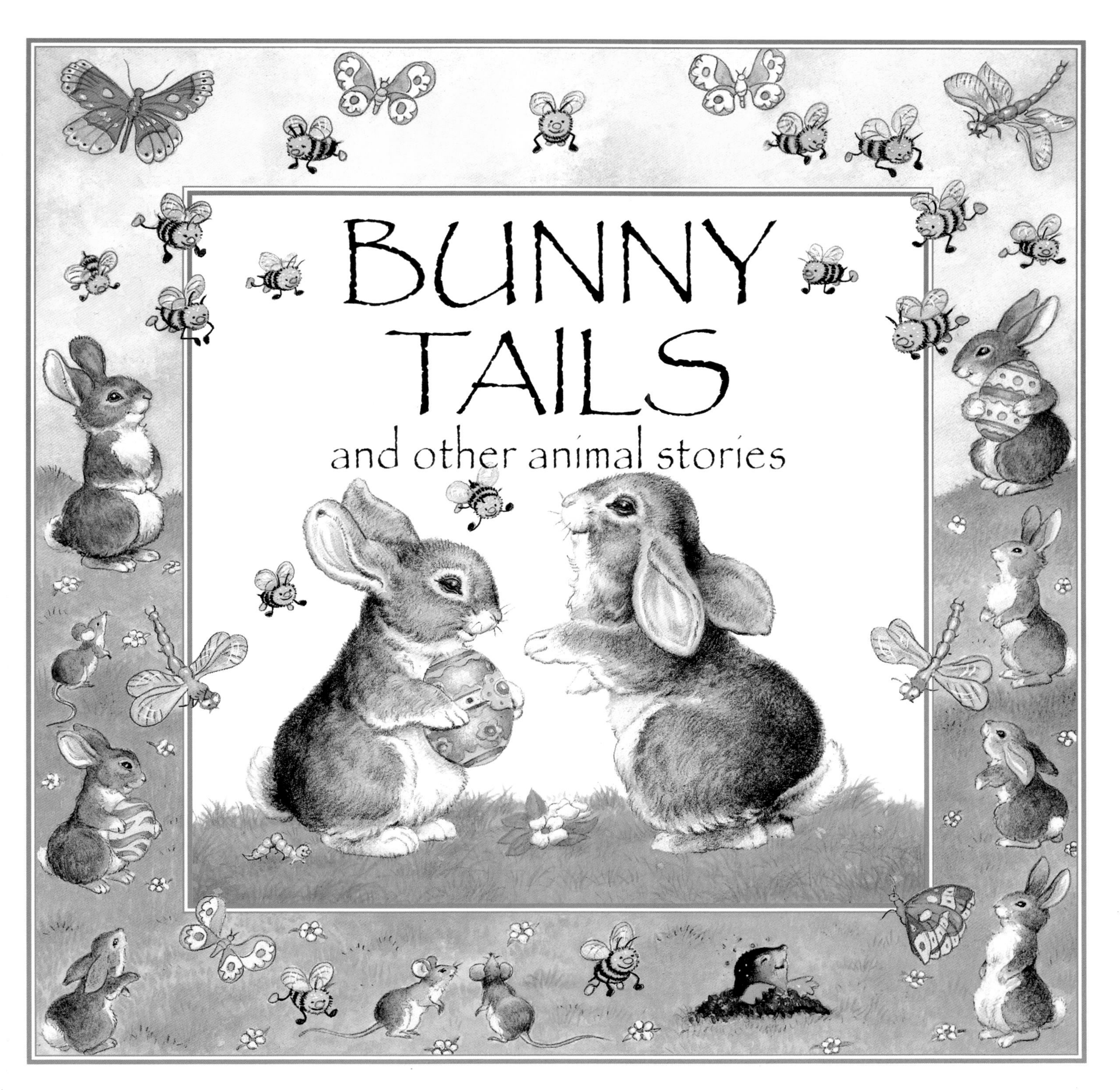

Written by Caroline Repchuk • Illustrated by Mario Capaldi and Stephanie Boey

CONTENTS

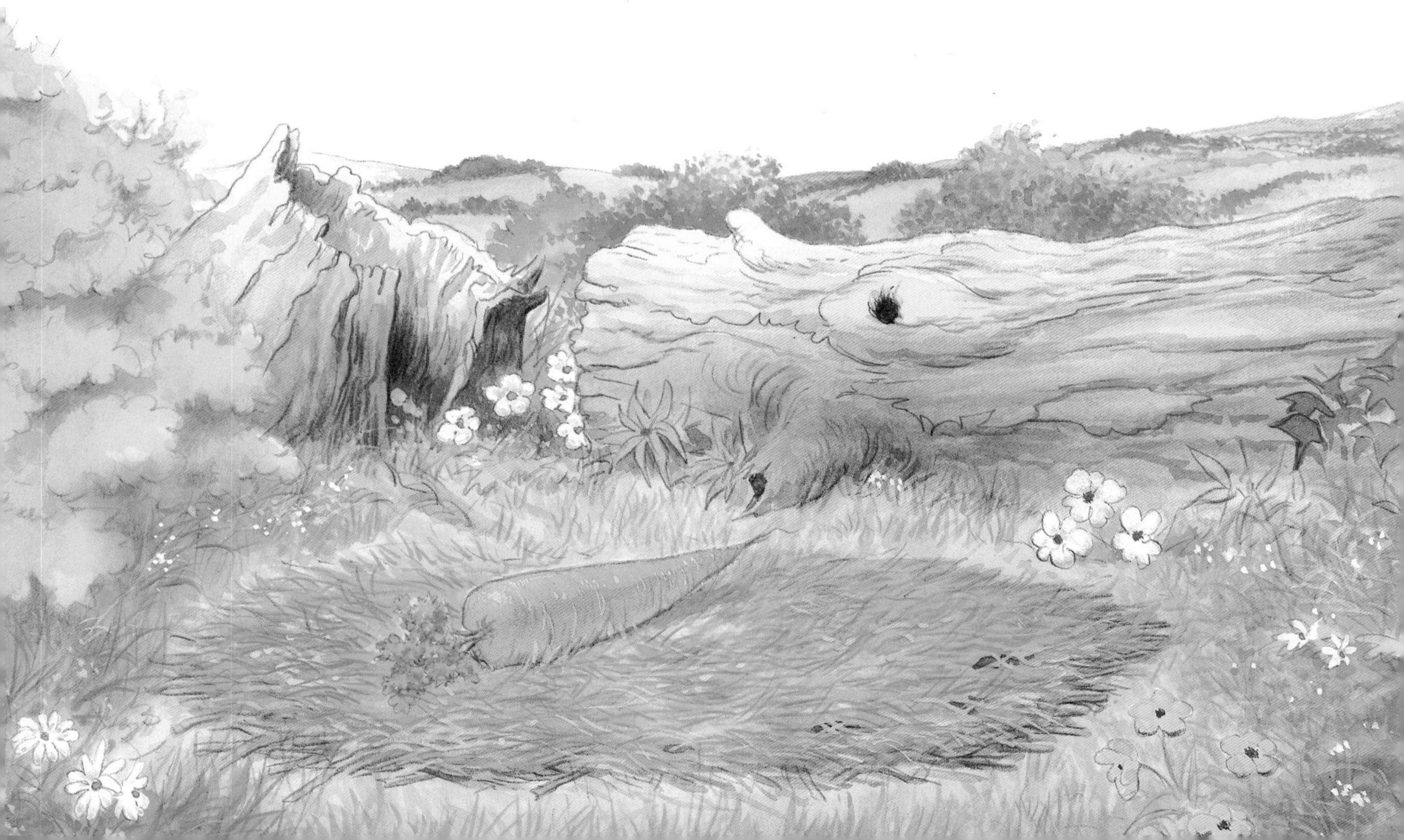

Like a Duck to Water

The Disappearing Trick

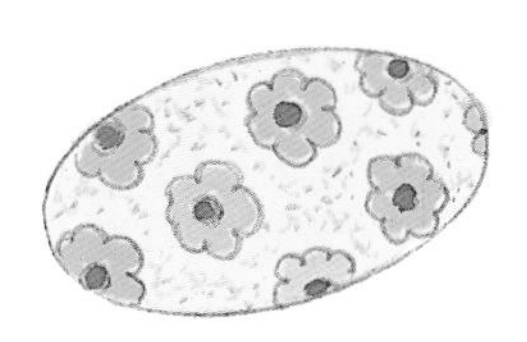

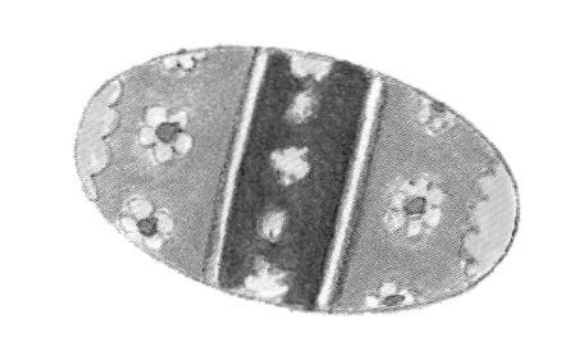

One Snowy Day

Bone Crazy

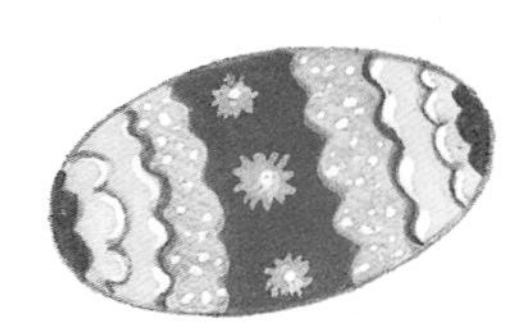

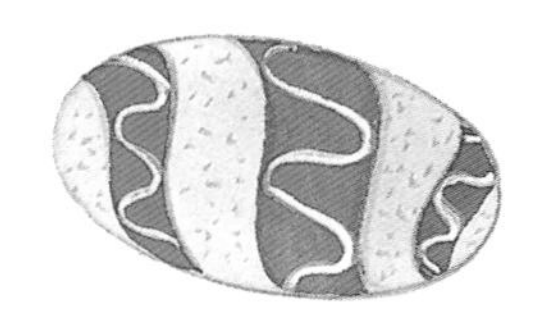

Easter Bunnies

Making a Splash

BUNNY TAILS

Bunnies come in all different colours and sizes. Some have long ears and some have floppy ears. But all bunnies have fluffy tails. All except Alfie, that is. He had no tail at all and his friends teased him badly. "Never mind, dear," said his mummy. "I love you, tail or no tail."

But Alfie did mind and at night he cried himself to sleep. Then one night he dreamt he met a fairy and told her all about his problem. "A little fairy magic will soon

fix that!" said the fairy. She took some dandelion clocks and sewed them together to make a lovely fluffy tail. "Turn around!" she said and fixed it in place in a flash.

Alfie woke with a start. "If only my dream could come true," he thought sadly and looked down at his back. And there, to his astonishment, was a fine fluffy white tail!

"I'm a real bunny at last!" he said proudly, running off to show his new tail to his friends.

Cheeky Chick

Cheeky Chick was a playful little chick. He was always playing tricks on his brothers and sisters. He would hide in the long grass, then jump out on them in surprise, shouting, "Boo!" One day they decided to get their own back. "Let's play hide and seek," they said.

They left Cheeky Chick to count to ten, while they all went to hide. Cheeky Chick hunted high and low for his brothers and sisters. He looked in all his favourite

hiding places but they were nowhere to be found. “Come out,” he called. “I give up!” But no one came.

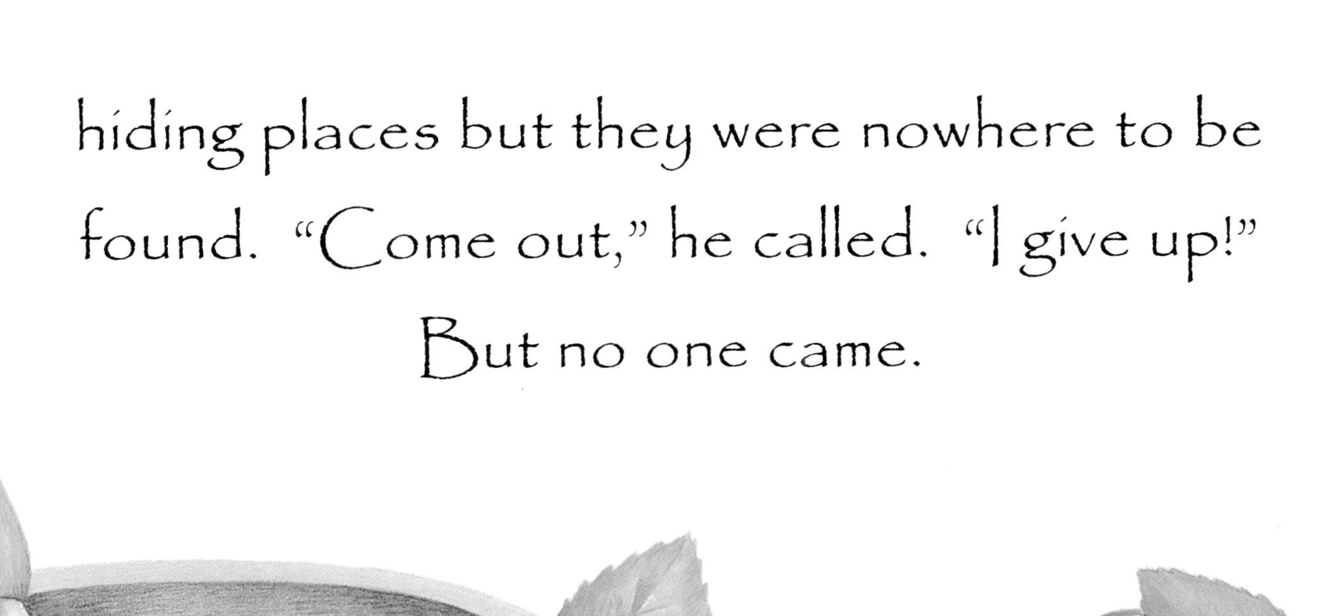

So Cheeky Chick carried on looking. He searched carefully all through the farmyard, through the vegetable patch and along the hedgerow at the edge of the field. He even looked in the haystack, which took a very long time, but there was no sign of his brothers and sisters to be found amongst the hay.

By now it was getting dark, and Cheeky Chick was feeling scared and lonely. "It's no use," he said to himself. "I'll have to go home." He hurried to the henhouse and opened the door. "Surprise!" came a loud chorus. His brothers and sisters had been hiding there all along! It was a long time before Cheeky Chick played tricks on them again.

Like A Duck To Water

Mrs Duck swam proudly across the farm pond followed by a line of fluffy ducklings. Hidden in the safety of the nest Dozy Duckling peeked out and watched them go. He wished he was brave enough to go with them but he was afraid of the water! Instead, he pretended to be asleep, and Mrs Duck told the others to leave him alone.

When they returned that night they told him tales of all the scary animals they had met by the pond. "There's a big thing with hot breath called Horse," said Dotty. "There's a huge smelly pink thing called Pig," said Dickie.

"But worst of all," said Doris, "there's a great grey bird, called Heron. Pig says he gobbles up little ducklings for breakfast!" At that all the little ducklings squawked with fear and excitement.

Next morning, Mrs Duck hurried the ducklings out for their morning parade. Dozy kept his eyes shut until they had gone then looked up to see a great grey bird towering over him! He leapt into the water crying, "Help, wait for me!" But the others started laughing! "It's a trick! Heron won't eat you. We just wanted you to come swimming. And you've taken to it like a duck to water!"

The Disappearing Trick

Like all little kittens, Smoky was very playful. One day, she was chasing her ball, when it rolled under the fence and into the garden on the other side. Forgetting Mummy's warnings about the mean dog who lived there, Smoky squeezed through the fence, just in time to see her ball disappear into a hole in the grass...

Smoky looked down into the hole, but it was very deep and there was no sign of the ball. Just then, she heard a low growl, and turned to see an angry dog snarling at her. In a flash, she scrambled into the hole,

with the dog's sharp teeth snapping at her heels. She squeezed down a long tunnel and into a little room at the bottom. "Hello!" said Rabbit, handing Smoky the ball. "You must be looking for this!"

Smoky was amazed to find she was in Rabbit's burrow. She told him about the angry dog. "Don't worry," said Rabbit, "we'll trick him!" He dug a new tunnel and in no time they were back in Smoky's garden. "Over here!" Rabbit called through the fence to the poor dog still guarding the hole! How the two friends laughed to see the puzzled look on his face.

One Snowy Day

One snowy day, Old Bear poked his nose out of his den, and looked at the deep snow that had fallen while he slept. "I'll take a stroll in the woods," he said. Off he went, his great paws padding along, as big white snowflakes tickled his nose. How he loved the snow! He walked far into the woods, deep in thought, and quite forgot to look where he was going.

After a while, Old Bear stopped and looked around. To his dismay, he realised he was quite lost. Then he spied the trail of pawprints behind him. "Ho, ho!" he chuckled. "I'm not lost at all! I can follow my pawprints home!"

And thinking what a clever old bear he was, he carried on walking, until at last he began to feel tired. "I'll just take a rest," he said to himself. He closed his eyes, and soon fell fast asleep. Meanwhile, the snow kept on falling...

By the time Old Bear woke up his trail of pawprints had disappeared! "Now I'll never find my way home!" he groaned. Then, he noticed an old tree stump nearby. "That looks familiar. And so does that fallen log over there. If I'm not mistaken, I've walked in a big circle, and ended up at home!" he chuckled, turning towards his den. "What a clever old bear I am, after all!"

BONE CRAZY!

Alfie sat in his basket chewing on a large bone. Mmm! It tasted good. When he had chewed it for long enough, he took it down to the bottom of the garden, to bury it in his favourite spot, beneath the old oak tree. He didn't see next door's dog, Ferdy, watching him through a hole in the fence.

The next day, when Alfie went to dig up his bone, it was gone! He dug all around, but it was nowhere to be found. Just then, he spied a trail of muddy paw prints leading to the fence, and he realised what had happened.

Alfie was too big to fit through the fence and get his bone back, so he thought of a plan, instead! Next day he buried another bone. This time, he knew Ferdy was watching him.

Later he hid and watched as Ferdy crept into the garden and started to dig up the bone. Just then, Ferdy yelped in pain. The bone had bitten his nose! He flew across the garden and through the fence leaving the bone behind. Alfie's friend Mole crept out from where the bone was buried. How the two friends laughed at their trick! And from then, Ferdy always kept safely to his side of the fence!

Easter Bunnies

It was Easter and the naughty bunnies had hidden eggs for the animals to find. How they chuckled when they saw the farm cat shaking the water from her fur. She had been searching by the pond and had fallen in!

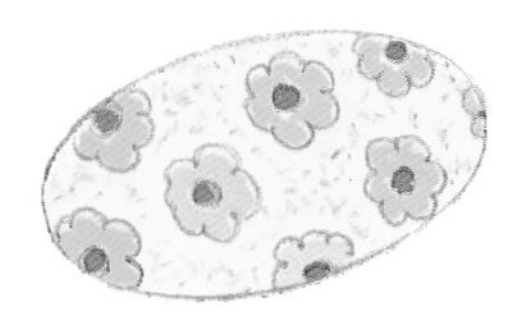
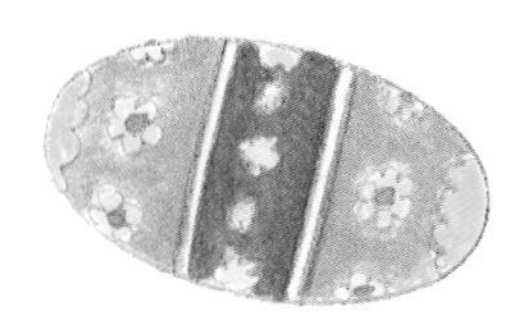

The bunnies giggled as they watched the hens shooing the pig away from the henhouse. "They're not in here!" the hens clucked.

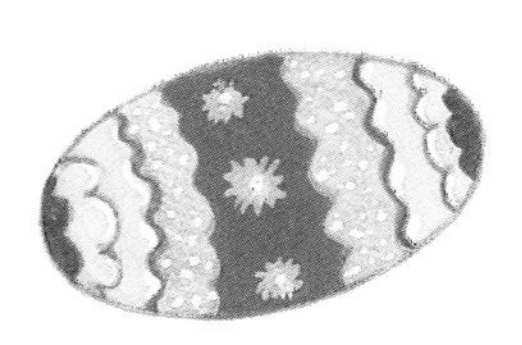

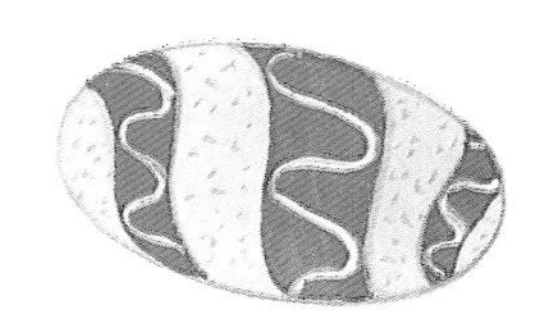

Next the little bunnies hurried to the meadow, where all the sheep were making a great fuss.

"We've found the Easter eggs!" cried the sheep, pointing behind a tree. "Those are toadstools!" laughed the bunnies. "Keep looking!" By now, the animals had searched high and low. "We give up!" said Daisy, the cow.

"Here's a clue," said the bunnies.
"Where do you find eggs?"
"In a nest," answered Mrs Goose.
"And what do you make a nest with?"
asked the bunnies.

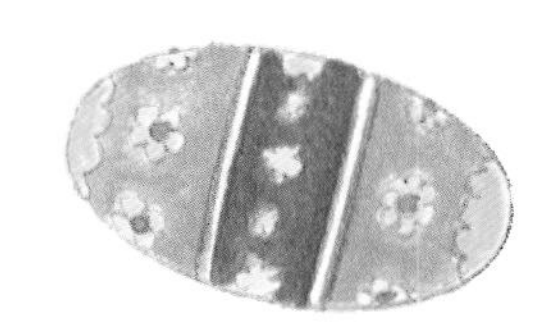

"Straw!" said the horse.
"They must be in the haystack!"
The animals rushed to the field and
there, hidden in the haystack, was a
pile of lovely Easter eggs.
What a feast they had!

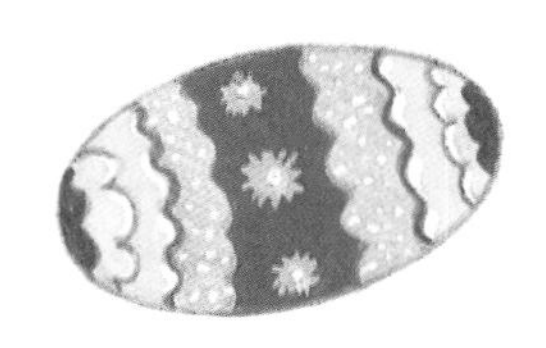
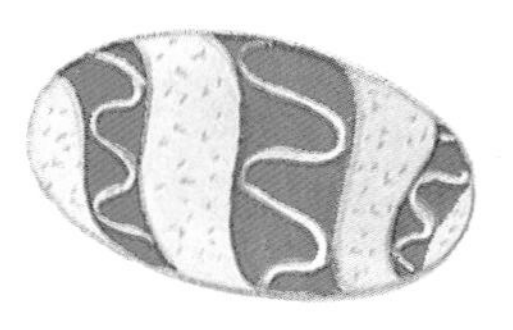

Making A Splash!

One day, Mrs Hen and her chicks were walking near the pond when Mrs Duck swam by, followed by a line of ducklings. The ducklings splashed around ducking and diving in the water. "Can we play in the water too?" the chicks asked Mrs Hen. "It looks like fun!"

"Oh, no, dears," said Mrs Hen. "Chicks and water don't mix!" This made the chicks very miserable. "It's not fair!" they grumbled. "We wish we were ducklings!" On the way home, a big black cloud appeared and it started to rain. Soon the chicks' fluffy feathers were wet through.

They scurried back to the henhouse as fast as they could and arrived wet, cold and shivering. Soon they were snuggled in the cosy warm straw, and their feathers were dry and fluffy again.

"Imagine being wet all the time!" said the chicks. "Thank goodness we're not ducklings, after all!"

The End